One of the great ironies of this life is this:
He or she who serves almost always
benefits more than he or she who is served.
-Gordon B. Hinckley

We are what we believe we are.
-C.S. Lewis

You are the only person on earth
who can use your ability.
-Zig Ziglar

Whether you feel like a hero or not,
you are one!

You are the hero of
your own life's story!
-Dieter F. Uchtdorf

We worry about what a child will
become tomorrow, yet we forget
that he is somone today.
-Stacia Tauscher

To know even one life has breathed
easier because you have lived.
This is to have succeeded.
-Attributed to Ralph Waldo Emerson

At times our light goes out and is
rekindled by a spark from another person.
Each of us has cause to think with
deep gratitude of those who have lighted
the flame within us.
-Albert Schweitzer

People who put the well-being
of others in front of themselves
are the most heroic and
thoughtful people I know.
-Mark Ruffalo

No pessimist ever discovered the
secrets of the stars, or sailed
to an uncharted land, or opened a
new heaven to the human spirit.
-Helen Keller

For all those who reached
out to Bridger when he was hurt...

You are our heroes!

You Can Be a Hero
by Robert and Teila Walker
Illustrated by Angelo France

Text copyright ©2024 by Robert and Teila Walker
Illustrations copyright © 2024 by Robert and Teila Walker
All rights reserved. Published by Forgotten Places Publishing LLC in Cheyenne, WY, USA

LCCN: 2024911975
ISBN 978-1-944621-31-5
First Edition

You Can Be a Hero

By Robert and Teila Walker

Illustrated by Angelo France

FORGOTTEN PLACES PUBLISHING

Cheyenne, WY

I want to be a hero like my brother is to me;

Somehow become the person he inspires me to be.

But I'm still little,
what can a kid really do?
Everything feels hard,
and I don't have a clue!

It seems a bit impossible
to save the world from doom
when I can barely clean
my itty bitty room!

I'm not fast, strong, or even very brave. This is not how I think a hero would behave!

What can I do
when I'm clearly falling short;
like when I lose my temper
or feel all out of sorts.

I know that
no one is perfect.
STRONG
HAS
MANY
FORMS

Everybody makes mistakes.

We have space to learn and grow when we give each other grace.

Maybe being a hero isn't out of reach at all...
IT DOESN'T MATTER WHAT YOU SAY IT MATTERS WHAT YOU DO.
49

There are things
that can be done,
even though I'm **small**.

I can **cheer** on others,
and **help** them reach their dreams.

When I help other people win,

I win too, it seems!
WIT
FINISH

I may not do it perfectly,
I'm sure I'll make a mess!
What matters most is the love that's shared
and the lives that I can bless.

I can't expect my first try
to be so very neat,
but I know I will get better if I
repeat, repeat, repeat.
SHINE YOUR LIGHT
22
34

So, when that little
voice inside whispers,
"help someone in need,"

I will try with all my heart
to do a kindly deed.

I won't just sit back
if something isn't right.
Even if it's hard or scary,
I'll try with all my might!

The task might seem overwhelming, but I can always ask for help! I cannot possibly do it all, all by my little self!
STAY WILD
BOSS
KING
OLD School
DISCIPLINE EQUALS FREEDOM

Everybody has a **talent**;
a **gift** they can pursue.

When we WORK together,
there's nothing we can't do!

YOU CAN BE A HERO
I suppose heroes don't have to be brave, fast, or strong!
Now I see by being me, I've been a hero all along!
So, I'll keep on scattering love along my way.
It's my hidden talent that will help me save the day!

And YOU
can be a HERO too!

This book is dedicated to the thousands of people who sent prayers, messages, cards, packages, rocks, love, support, and much much more to Bridger and our family when he was hurt. You restored our faith in humanity and gave us hope for a bright future when things seemed very bleak.

See if you can find the little tokens ("easter eggs") that we put throughout the book as a special thank you to the following people/groups. There's no way we could include everyone who made such a huge impact, but we figured we had to start somewhere.

49ers	Marcus Lemonis
Anne Hathaway	Mark Ruffalo
Apeman Strong	Mr. Beast
Bo Jackson	One More Level
Brett Michaels	Operation Underground Railroad (OUR)
Brothers Trust	Paul Rudd
Chris Evans	Police/Military/Firefighters
Chris Hemsworth	Professional Bull Riding (PBR)
Chris Pratt	Rener Gracie
Clymb - Abu Dhabi	Robert Downey Jr.
Dr. Dhaval Bhanusali	Rocks/ Gems Enthusiasts
Dr. (Pimple Popper) Sandra Lee	Tap Cancer Out
Dude Dad	Tom Holland
Etihad Airways	Water World - Abu Dhabi
FYI Yachts	World Boxing Council (WBC)
Ferrari World - Yas Island	Yas Island
Jocko Willink	Zachary Levi
Jui-Jitsu Dummies	Zendaya
Larry Nance	

Discussion Questions

1. What does it mean to be a hero?

2. Brielle discovered that her super power is spreading love wherever she goes. In what ways did the other characters show they were heroes too?

3. There is a heart hidden in every scene representing Brielle's super power. Did you find them all?

4. When Wit broke the bank, what did he do?

5. What does it mean to give someone grace?

6. How does staying positive help us deal with tough situations?

7. What do you think Bridger told Brielle before the scooter race?

8. Bridger is Brielle's hero and somebody she looks up to. Who is your hero and why?

9. What are your super powers?

10. What is something you could do today to make your family or community better?

Meet the Characters

A hero is someone who protects and helps people, and sometimes when people really need help a hero stands up for them. Bridger saved my life and he's a hero!
Brielle Walker (8)

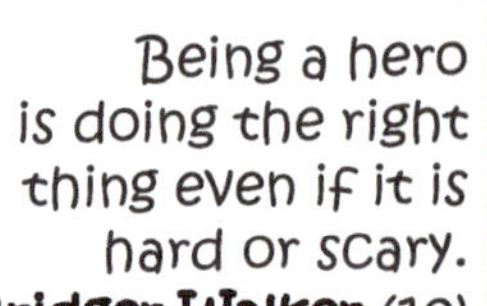

Being a hero is doing the right thing even if it is hard or scary.
Bridger Walker (10)

A hero is someone who loves and cares about others.
Johnny Walker (13)

I think a hero is someone who willingly cares for others and helps when needed. Not for attention, but because they genuinely love and care.
Mylee Walker (16)

A hero is saving the day!
Wit Walker (5)

About the Authors

Robert Walker is a practicing attorney and co-founder of the firm Walker Law. Born and raised in Cheyenne, Wyoming, he spent 2 years serving a mission in Brazil and is fluent in Portuguese.

www.instagram.com/
RobertWalker307

Growing up, **Teila Walker** lived in several countries including Mexico, USA, and Ukraine. Teila has a degree in Family and Consumer Sciences and taught Culinary Arts and Early Childhood Development at the high school level prior to becoming a stay at home mom. www.instagram.com/TeilaWalker

Robert and Teila have been married for 19 years and have 5 children. They enjoy traveling and creating new experiences with their kids.

About the Illustrator

Angelo France is a 45 year old illustrator born in Campinas, Sao Paulo Brazil, specializing in digital illustration.

He's married to Eveline, and is the father to an intelligent and creative 9 year old boy named Alex.

The book "You Can Be a Hero" is the 4th book he has illustrated to be published.

Angelo France's work can be found at:
www.instagram.com/AngeloFrance

Frequently Asked Questions

Q. **Is Bridger afraid of dogs?**
A. Not any more! It took time and a lot of work, but we are so proud of Bridger for facing his fears.

Q. **What did your family do to help Bridger overcome his fear of dogs?**
A. It helped that we had dogs at home that Bridger already knew and loved. He has also always loved animals, so he didn't want to be afraid. Bridger had mentioned that he didn't understand why the dog attacked. It left him feeling uncertain, so we hired a dog trainer to work with him and help him understand dogs' body language and behavior. When he was ready, we started introducing him to calm, well-trained dogs and tiny puppies. Eventually he started asking for a puppy of his own. He was gifted a beautiful pup by @realchicolopez, (therealpitbull.com). He named her Cyborg after his favorite MMA fighter, Chris Cyborg. Training Cyborg (with help from his parents), has given Bridger a much needed sense of control, and they are best friends.

Q. **Why would you get Bridger a pitbull?!?!**
A. Bridger met Athos (Cyborg's father) at a boxing event and absolutely loved him. When he learned Athos had just sired a litter of puppies, he began asking for one. We were very hesitant, but after a lot of research we learned that over the years, the term "pitbull" has come to encompass a wide variety of breeds, many of which are more mixed breed than actual pitbull. Cyborg is a pure American Pitbull Terrier, a breed known for their outgoing, friendly personality and eagerness to please people. Our concern was especially alleviated after learning that the American Veterinary Medical Association conducted studies that found breed to be an unreliable indicator of dangerous behavior in dogs. Owner behavior, training, sex, neuter status, and living conditions were found to be more reliable indicators. Furthermore, Cyborg's breeder, Chico Lopez, has more than 30 years of experience and has stated that none of his dogs have ever bitten a human - a testament to the quality of his dogs, and the care he takes to place them in good homes.

Q. **What do you wish you could share with families to help protect them against dog bites?**
A. We would love for more families to understand that EVERY dog is capable of biting, even your beloved family pet that has always been great with children. After Bridger's experience, we have heard from many other dog bite victims, most of which said the attack came from a family dog, and they never would have expected it. Dogs are more likely to bite when stressed, eating, in pain, or even just meeting people for the first time. It can be hard to tell what a dog is feeling, so it is important to be familiar with the signs indicating stress, fear, aggression, or pain. We wish every family could understand the importance of training their dog, teaching their children how to interact appropriately, and especially staying vigilant when introducing children to a new dog. There are a lot of free resources online to help with training and understanding behavior.

Q. **How is Bridger doing now?**
A. Bridger is doing great! He still has some general anxiety, but for the most part, is a happy, active and social kid. He loves sports, particularly soccer, jui jitsu, and boxing. He also loves video games, science, and rocks.

Q. **Where can we go to get updates on how Bridger and Brielle are doing?**
A. The family posts occasional updates on Instagram (@robertwalker307, @teilawalker), YouTube (BridgerBuddies), and bridgerwalker.com.

Q. **How can we contact the family regarding speaking engagements and other inquiries?**
A. The family can be reached at bridgerstrong307@gmail.com